Anna
the Arctic Fox
Fairy

by Daisy Meadows

ORCHARD

www.rainbowmagic.co.uk

The Fairyland Palace

Meadow

Stream

Beehive

Arctic Tundra

Eucalyptus Forest

Tropical Waterfall

Jack Frost's
Ice Castle

To Jack Frost's Zoo ↗

Wild Woods
Nature
Reserve

Watering Hole

Pagoda

Desert Oasis

Jack Frost's Spell

I love animals, yes I do,
I want my very own private zoo!
I'll capture the animals one by one,
With fairy magic to help me on!

A koala, a tiger, an Arctic fox,
I'll keep them in cages with giant locks.
Every kind of animal will be there,
A panda, a meerkat, a honey bear.
The animals will be my property,
I'll be master of a huge menagerie!

Contents

Moonlight Magic

"Isn't it a beautiful evening?" Rachel Walker remarked to her best friend, Kirsty Tate, glancing up at the night sky strewn with tiny, glittering stars. The evening air was warm and still, and above the trees the moon shone with a pale, silvery light.

"It's a lovely way to end our week at Wild Woods," Kirsty agreed. The girls had volunteered to spend part of their summer holidays at the nature reserve near Kirsty's home, learning how to be junior rangers. Now it was their last day, and all the volunteers were waiting outside the wildlife centre for Becky, the manager of Wild Woods, to join them for a special evening.

"It's really kind of Becky to take us on a night-time walk," Rachel said. "I hope we see lots of different animals."

"Becky said it was a special treat because we'd all worked so hard," Kirsty reminded her, "although we *do* have our badges as well!"

Both girls gazed proudly at the pockets of their backpacks, which were covered with badges. Every time they'd completed their tasks successfully, Becky had given them a badge, and the girls had six so far.

There was a murmur of excitement as Becky hurried out of the wildlife centre, carrying a bag of equipment.

"Well, we have a wonderful evening for our walk," Becky said. "But to make the most of it, you'll all need one of *these*!" She took a torch out of the bag and switched it on. Rachel and Kirsty were surprised to see the torch glow red.

"These torches have special red filters that allow you to see in the dark," Becky went on, handing the torches out. "But they won't disturb wildlife like a bright yellow beam would. So keep your eyes peeled for animals that only come out at night!"

"And we should keep our eyes peeled for fairies, too!" Kirsty whispered to Rachel, excitedly.

Alongside working at the nature reserve, the girls had also been helping the seven Baby Animal Rescue Fairies protect wildlife from Jack Frost and his naughty goblins. When Rachel and Kirsty arrived at Wild Woods, they'd

been delighted to meet their old friend
from Fairyland, Bertram the frog
footman. Bertram had taken them to
visit the Fairyland Nature Reserve, but
Jack Frost and his goblins turned up
to spoil everyone's fun. Jack Frost had
announced that he wanted animals
for a zoo at his Ice Castle! With one
bolt of icy magic from his wand, he'd
stolen the Baby Animal Rescue Fairies'
magical, animal-shaped key rings. Then
Jack Frost had given the key rings to his
goblins and sent them spinning away to
the human world with strict orders to
collect animals for his zoo.

Rachel and Kirsty had offered to help
the Baby Animal Rescue Fairies get
their key rings back, so the fairies had
combined their remaining magic to give

the girls the power to talk to animals.

"It's been huge fun talking to all the animals we've met," Rachel said as everyone followed Becky into the woods. "And the magic has helped us rescue six baby animals from Jack Frost and his goblins, too."

"Now we only have Anna the Arctic Fox Fairy's key ring to find," Kirsty pointed out. "Then all wildlife will be safe from Jack Frost, and the animals won't end up in his private zoo!"

"Let's stay a little behind the others," Rachel suggested. "Just in case we *do* meet a fairy!"

Becky led the junior rangers down a winding path through the trees, Kirsty and Rachel bringing up the rear. Suddenly they heard a hooting noise.

"Hoo! Hoo!"

"An owl!" Becky declared, her eyes gleaming with excitement. "Keep still, everyone."

Seconds later a brown and white owl swooped past them, amber eyes glinting in the moonlight. Everyone gasped with delight.

The owl landed in a tree near the girls, and peered down at them.

"Lovely evening," the owl hooted softly.

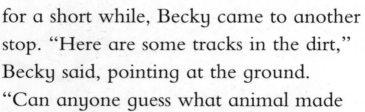

"Yes, it is," Kirsty murmured, hoping the others wouldn't hear.

After walking for a short while, Becky came to another stop. "Here are some tracks in the dirt," Becky said, pointing at the ground. "Can anyone guess what animal made these footprints?"

The junior rangers gathered around her. Rachel and Kirsty were about to join them when they heard a noise in the bushes close by.

"It was *me* who made those tracks!" whispered a deep voice.

Rachel shone her torch into the undergrowth. The girls saw a badger snuffling around in the leaves, his big eyes bright in the moonlight.

"Oh, hello!" Kirsty said.

"Good evening," the badger replied, scurrying busily away.

"We'd better go," Rachel said,
noticing that Becky and the others had
walked on.

Rachel switched off her torch, but
as she did so, Kirsty spotted a flash of
something glittering in the moonlight,
deep in the undergrowth. Kirsty
wondered if it was another animal. But,
if so, what on earth could it be?

"Rachel, there's something sparkly
among the leaves!" Kirsty whispered.

This time both girls turned their torches on. And there, in the red glow, they saw Anna the Arctic Fox Fairy perched on a twig right in front of them!

Paw Prints in the Snow

"Have you been expecting me, girls?" Anna cried, twirling up into the air. She wore a blue dress printed with red hearts, a snug white fur gilet and fur-trimmed boots. The ends of her long blonde hair were dip-dyed gorgeous shades of pink and purple.

"We *have* been looking out for you,

Anna," Kirsty
replied.

"We only
have one key
ring left to find
now," Anna
said, landing
on Rachel's
shoulder. "*Mine!*
Girls, I need your
help. A little fox cub
called Dazzle has gone missing. I don't
know if Jack Frost has anything to do
with her disappearance, but we *must* find
Dazzle and bring her safely home."

"Of course!" Kirsty replied. "We're
ready!" The girls switched off their
torches and with one flick of Anna's
wand, fairy sparkles floated gently down

around them. Then Rachel and Kirsty were lifted off their feet and swept far away from Wild Woods.

Just a heartbeat later, the girls found themselves in an icy, frozen land. The snow-covered ground glittered beneath the moonlit sky, and a harsh wind was blowing, whipping up flurries of snowflakes in the distance.

"Where are we?" Kirsty asked. She was glad that Anna's magic had provided both girls with hooded parkas, fur-lined boots and cosy hats, scarves and mittens.

"I thought foxes lived in forests or fields," Rachel added, puzzled. She couldn't see a single tree or plant anywhere on the frozen landscape.

"Girls, this is the Arctic tundra," Anna explained. "Arctic foxes live near the North Pole, and the ground is frozen here for most of the year. Nothing much can grow."

Kirsty could see something imprinted in the thick snow around her feet. "These are paw prints," she said, looking more closely. "And they're quite small, too. I wonder what animal made them?"

"Let's follow the trail," Anna suggested.

The girls walked across the crisp, deep snow, Anna flying alongside. After a few moments they arrived at a mound of snow with a small hole dug in the side.

"This is a fox's den," Anna told them.

"I think Dazzle and her family live here. Let's go inside."

Anna shook her wand and a few fairy sparkles, shining brightly against the white snow, tumbled gently down onto Rachel and Kirsty. Immediately the girls began to shrink, stopping only when they were the exact same size as Anna herself.

The three of them flew into the foxhole. As they moved along the

network of tunnels, going deeper underground, Kirsty was surprised how warm and sheltered it felt beneath the blanket of thick snow.

At last they reached the den. Rachel exclaimed in delight as she spotted four fox cubs cuddled together, their long, fluffy tails curled neatly around them. The cubs had thick fur, as white as the snow, and adorable little faces with small pink noses and bright black eyes.

"Hello, cubs," Anna said. "Has Dazzle come home yet?"

The cubs looked worried.

"No, she hasn't," the biggest cub squeaked anxiously.

"And we can't tell our mum because she's out hunting," added one of the others.

"We'll find Dazzle and bring her home," Anna told the fox cubs.

"Thank you!" they squeaked in chorus.

Anna and the girls said goodbye to the fox cubs and then set off along the maze of tunnels again. When they reached the surface, Kirsty zoomed out of the hole first, only to be hit by a swirling mass of snow that knocked the breath out of her.

"Oh!" Kirsty gasped, realising it had begun snowing heavily while they

were inside the
hole. She tried
to flutter upwards
but the snow was
falling so thickly,
it was impossible
to fly. The huge
snowflakes
knocked Kirsty out
of the air, forcing her
to land on the ground. Rachel
and Anna fought their way through the
blizzard and joined her.

"What are we going to do?" Rachel
panted despairingly, shaking the snow
from her hood. "How on earth are we
going to find Dazzle if we can barely get
off the ground?"

Sleigh Ride

Kirsty, Rachel and Anna stared at each other in dismay. Then, to her surprise, Kirsty heard the sound of jingling bells, followed by the noise of dogs yapping.

"Someone's coming!" Kirsty said breathlessly.

Rachel peered through the whirling snowflakes and saw a wooden sleigh pulled by dogs skimming across the snow.

A young Inuit boy dressed in warm, fur-trimmed clothes was holding the dogs' reins, urging them on.

"Maybe he can help us," Rachel suggested eagerly.

Anna nodded. "Quickly, girls, let me turn you back to your human size before he disappears!" she said.

The girls immediately ducked behind a snowdrift so that Anna could work

her magic. Then they waded out again,
hoping the boy hadn't gone very far. To
Rachel's relief, she saw that the sleigh
had stopped nearby.

"Good luck, girls," Anna told them.
"I'd better hide!"

Rachel tucked the little fairy safely
inside her woolly scarf. Then she and
Kirsty hurried through the falling snow
towards the
boy. He was
speaking to
his dogs,
patting their
heads one
by one.

"Hello!" Kirsty
called, brushing the
snowflakes from her nose.

The boy turned and gazed at them in surprise. "Hello," he replied. "I wasn't expecting to meet anyone! Who are you?"

"I'm Rachel, and this is Kirsty," Rachel explained.

"I'm Miko," the boy said, his dark eyes warm and friendly. "I'm going to visit my grandmother, but I think something's wrong with one of my dogs."

Kirsty glanced at the dogs. They had thick brown and white fur and curling tails, and they looked fit and strong, but Kirsty could hear one of them whimpering softly.

"Oh, my paw really hurts!"

Rachel heard it too, and she and Kirsty exchanged a knowing glance.

"Maybe I could check the dogs for you, Miko," Kirsty suggested.

"Thank you," Miko said gratefully.

While Kirsty went to find the injured dog, Rachel stayed with Miko. "This place is amazing," Rachel said as more snow settled around them, glittering like white diamonds in the silver moonlight.

"There's so much snow and ice! Does it ever melt?"

"Yes, in summer the snow disappears," Miko explained. "Summer days are very short here, but the sun shines all the time, even at midnight!"

"That's amazing!" Rachel gasped.

"Something even more amazing happens here in winter," Miko told her. "If you're lucky, you can see the Northern Lights!"

"The Northern Lights?" Rachel repeated.

"It's a big, colourful display of lights in the night sky," Miko said. "My dad explained to me exactly how nature makes the Northern Lights happen, but I just like to think of it as something magical and beautiful."

By now Kirsty had found
the whimpering dog.
She knelt down
beside him.

"What's the
matter?" Kirsty
whispered, concerned.

"I have something stuck in my paw,"
the dog panted, holding up one of his
front legs. "Please help me!"

Gently Kirsty checked the dog's
paw and straight away she spotted a
sharp sliver of ice stuck in his soft pad.
Grasping the ice with her mittened hand,
she eased it out carefully.

"Thank you!" the dog barked.

"Your dog's fine now," Kirsty called
to Miko. "He had some ice stuck in his
paw, but I've taken it out."

"Poor Shika!" Miko hurried over to pat the dog. "Thank you, Kirsty. I'm sure Shika would say thank you, too, if he could."

Kirsty laughed. "Yes, I'm sure he would!" she agreed.

"Now, is there anything I can do to help *you*?" Miko asked. "I see you don't have a sleigh. Can I take you somewhere?"

"We're searching for a missing fox cub," Kirsty explained. "Would you help us look for her?"

"Of course!" Miko agreed eagerly.

Then Rachel heard Anna whispering urgently to her from inside her scarf.

"Rachel, look – in the distance!"

The snow had stopped falling now and Rachel could see across the frozen plain.

There, silhouetted against the stark white
landscape, she could see another sleigh
whizzing along. This sleigh was nothing
like Miko's simple wooden sledge,
though – it was blue, and much more
ornate. Rachel could see that the sleigh
was decorated with glittering icicles
twisted into fantastical shapes. The driver
was wearing a coat with a fur-trimmed
hood pulled over his face as if to disguise
himself, but Rachel could see he was tall
and thin with a long nose and
a frozen beard.

"Look, Kirsty, it's Jack Frost!" Rachel gasped. "I bet he's kidnapped Dazzle!"

"Let's go after him!" Miko cried.

Rachel and Kirsty jumped onto the sleigh behind Miko. He gathered up the reins and called out to the dogs, who immediately took off, pulling the sleigh along with them. Kirsty gasped as the freezing wind whirled around them, reddening her cheeks. She was

utterly amazed at the speed they were travelling as they glided smoothly across the snow, the dogs running as fast as they could.

"We're catching up!" Rachel said as they drew nearer to Jack Frost's sleigh.

As Miko got closer to Jack Frost, Kirsty leaned forward to look into the other sleigh. She caught a glimpse of a ball of white fur on the seat next to Jack Frost.

"It's Dazzle!" Kirsty gasped.

Dazzle in Distress

"STOP!" Rachel yelled at the top of her voice. "Let that little fox cub go!" Jack Frost turned and shot her a freezing glare but he didn't stop.

"No way!" Jack Frost roared, so loudly he scared Miko's dogs and they all started barking. "My useless goblins were rubbish at collecting animals, so I've decided to get one for myself! And an

Arctic fox is the perfect creature for the zoo at my Ice Castle!"

"What's he saying?" Miko asked, "I can't hear because of the dogs."

"He wants the fox cub for his zoo," Kirsty explained.

"His zoo?" Miko exclaimed, shocked. "That's terrible!"

"How can we get Dazzle back,

Kirsty?" Rachel murmured as Jack Frost yelled at his dogs to go faster.

Kirsty thought hard as Miko's dogs, unsettled by Jack Frost, continued to bark noisily. Suddenly the dogs themselves gave her an idea.

"Rachel, I'm sure Jack Frost's dogs would stop if we told them their master had kidnapped a little fox cub!" Kirsty whispered hopefully. "But we'd have to do it without Miko seeing that we can talk to animals."

"Great idea," Rachel agreed. "I'm sure we could distract Miko somehow…" She suddenly remembered her conversation with Miko earlier and smiled. "And I think I know how!"

Quickly Rachel unwrapped her scarf and Anna peeked out.

"Miko told me the Northern Lights are magical and amazing," Rachel went on. "And I'm sure they'd distract him while we try to rescue Dazzle!"

"Let's see what I can do," Anna murmured, pointing her wand at the black night sky.

The girls watched a shower of dazzling sparks burst from the wand like an exploding firework. Immediately great ribbons of green light tinted with pink and violet formed across the sky, swirling and dancing in the darkness like giant flames.

"Look, Miko!" Rachel shouted, pointing at the sky.

"It's the Northern Lights!" Miko gasped excitedly, slowing the sleigh down to get a better look.

"Let's go, girls," Anna murmured. One wave of her wand transformed Rachel and Kirsty into fairies once more, and then they zoomed off towards Jack Frost's sleigh, while Miko stopped and gazed in awe at the spectacular lights above them.

Jack Frost had also slowed down a little to enjoy the magical display. He was so entranced, he didn't notice the fairies fly past him. "This light show must have been put on in my honour!" Rachel heard him murmuring boastfully.

Anna and the girls flew to hover above the dogs pulling the sleigh.

"Please stop!" Kirsty begged them. "Your master has kidnapped a baby animal!"

"*Kidnapped*?" all the dogs barked

together in amazement, and they came
to a dead halt. They stopped so suddenly
that Jack Frost was almost thrown out of
the sleigh.

"Come on, move!" Jack Frost shouted,
shaking the reins. "MOVE!" But the
dogs stayed where they were. Grumbling
loudly, Jack Frost climbed out of the
sleigh, leaving Dazzle huddled
miserably on
the seat.

"Let the fox cub go!" one of the dogs
yelped, and the others barked loudly in
agreement.

"You dogs are as useless as my silly
goblins!" Jack Frost clapped his hands
over his icy ears.

As Jack Frost continued to rant at
the dogs, Anna flew silently over to the
sleigh to check on Dazzle. Kirsty and

Rachel were following her when Kirsty glanced down and spotted something furry sticking out of one of the pockets of Jack Frost's coat.

"It's Anna's magical key ring!" Kirsty whispered to Rachel.

"Let's grab it!" Rachel suggested.

The Seventh Key Ring

The girls fluttered down behind Jack Frost so that he couldn't see them.

"How dare you disobey me!" Jack Frost shrieked at the dogs. He was having a tantrum now and stamping his foot in the snow. "I *order* you to move!"

"Not until you let the fox cub go," the lead dog barked.

Kirsty and Rachel hovered beside Jack Frost's pocket. They were so close to Anna's furry, fox-shaped key ring, they could see the faint magical glow that surrounded it.

"NOW!" Kirsty whispered. She and Rachel darted forward and together they lifted the key ring gently out of Jack Frost's pocket. Carrying it between them, they whizzed straight over to Anna who was talking softly to a dejected Dazzle. Anna stared at the key ring as if she couldn't believe her eyes, and her face lit up with pure joy.

"Aren't you clever, girls!" she declared. "Wherever did you find it?"

"In Jack Frost's pocket!" Rachel replied as she and Kirsty handed the key ring over. The very second Anna touched it, the key ring magically shrank to its fairy-size.

"I want my mummy," Dazzle squeaked. "I don't like that frosty man!"

"We'll take you home to your mummy, Dazzle," Anna told her. She showed the fox cub her key ring and Dazzle cheered up immediately when she saw its magical glow. Eagerly she jumped out of the sleigh. But unfortunately, at that moment Jack Frost happened to glance round. His face darkened when he spotted Anna, Rachel and Kirsty.

"I'm fed up with fairies!" Jack Frost roared. "Always following me around, sticking your nose into my business!" He charged towards them, trying to swat Anna and the girls away. "And keep your hands off that fox cub — she's going to be the prize exhibit in my special zoo!"

Skilfully Anna, Rachel and Kirsty avoided Jack Frost's flailing arms and flew back towards Miko's sleigh. Dazzle also dodged Jack Frost and scampered after them, her eyes fixed on the key ring Anna was holding. Miko was still gazing rapturously up at the colourful display in the sky and didn't even notice when Dazzle jumped into his sleigh. Then Anna waved her wand and her magic quickly restored the girls to their normal size.

"I'm tired of you
fairies always
messing everything
up!" Jack Frost
howled,
stomping
around in
frustration
and kicking
snow everywhere.

"You shouldn't have tried to steal
animals for your horrid old zoo, then!"
said Rachel.

"Animals aren't things to be collected,"
Kirsty reminded him. "They have to be
treated properly."

"Oh, how very boring!" Jack Frost
sneered. "Why do you fairies *always*
have to spoil *all* my fun?" And, still

complaining, he vanished in a shower of
icy magic. Smiling happily, Rachel and
Kirsty climbed into Miko's sleigh.

"Thank you for your help, girls," Anna
said gratefully, landing on Rachel's
shoulder. She pointed her wand up at the
sky again and, as the
lights began to fade,
she burrowed down
into Rachel's scarf,
out of sight.

"That was the
most amazing
Northern Lights
display I've ever seen!"
Miko turned to look at the girls, his
eyes wide with excitement. "It was so
magical, I even thought I saw some
fairies flitting about in the night sky!"

"Oh, it was probably just snowflakes you saw," Rachel said quickly.

"Or maybe it was us!" Kirsty whispered in her ear.

Then Miko noticed Dazzle on the seat next to him. "And you found the missing fox cub!" he exclaimed, stroking Dazzle's thick fur. "Shall we take her home?"

"Yes, please!" Dazzle squeaked.

"Yes, please, Miko," Rachel said, winking at Kirsty.

Swiftly Miko released Jack Frost's dogs and hitched them to his own sleigh. Then they sped off across the snowy plain, back towards the den. As they got nearer, Dazzle began to get very excited.

"Hurrah!" she shouted. "I'm going home!"

Miko stopped the sleigh outside the den

and Dazzle, Rachel and Kirsty jumped out together.

"I must go straight to my grandmother's," Miko said. "I'm very late. Goodbye to you all!"

Rachel and Kirsty thanked Miko and waved as the boy shot away across the snow. Then Dazzle raced towards the hole, but before she reached it, her brothers and sisters came tumbling out. They were followed by their mother, home from hunting.

"Dazzle's home!" the cubs chorused, rushing to nuzzle noses with their sister.

"Thank you *so* much," the mother fox said, as Dazzle nestled against her. "I've been very worried about her."

"She's quite safe now," Anna told them. "And I'll see you again very soon!" She turned to the girls and raised her wand. "Now, I think we should go back to the Fairyland Nature Reserve and tell everyone we've found my key ring at last!"

As Dazzle and her family called goodbye, a flash of sparkles from Anna's wand encircled Rachel and Kirsty, carrying them swiftly away from the snowy land. In the twinkling of an eye, the girls and Anna arrived at the Fairyland Nature Reserve where a

crowd had gathered to meet them. All
the other Baby Animal Rescue Fairies
were there, as well as King Oberon and
Queen Titania, and Rachel and Kirsty
were also delighted to see Bertram the
frog footman, Fluffy the squirrel and
Queenie the bee.

"Look!" cried Kitty the Tiger Fairy. "Anna has her key ring back which means our magic is complete once more!"

"Now we can protect wildlife everywhere again," Mae the Panda Fairy said happily.

There were cheers and everyone applauded loudly. Then Queen Titania stepped forward. "Girls, we must thank you for coming to our rescue," she said with a sweet smile. "You have proved yourself true friends over and over again."

"We're glad we could help," Rachel told her. "And we *did* have lots of fun talking to the animals!"

"Yes, we really loved it," Kirsty added. "But we know the magic can't last now that all the Baby Animal Rescue Fairies have their key rings back again."

"Well, maybe the magic can last for a *little* while longer," the queen replied. "Long enough for you two girls to join us for a celebration party with the animals here at the Fairyland Nature Reserve, maybe?"

There were more cheers as the girls glanced at each other in delight.

"We'd love to!" said Rachel.

"And thank you very much, Your Majesty!" Kirsty added.

Farewell to Wild Woods

The party at the Fairyland Nature
Reserve was so enchanting, Rachel and
Kirsty really didn't want to leave. The
Party Fairies had done all the organising.
They'd decorated the nature reserve with
lanterns and candles, and they'd hung
sparkly bunting in the trees. The Music
Fairies played beautiful music, and there
was a huge table laid with delicious

food, including seven spectacular iced
cakes shaped like the Baby Animal
Rescue Fairies' key rings. The girls had
a wonderful time dancing with the fairies
and chatting with the different animals
who all came to thank them for helping
to keep them safe.

But at last it was time for the girls to
return to Wild Woods, and everyone
gathered to see them off.

"Once again, girls, all our thanks,"
King Oberon said warmly. "Enjoy
the rest of your last evening at Wild
Woods!"

"We will!" Rachel said.

"Goodbye, everyone," Kirsty called
as Queen Titania pointed her wand at
them.

"Goodbye! Goodbye!" With the shouts
of their fairy friends ringing in their
ears, the girls were whisked away by
the queen's magic. Almost instantly they
found themselves back in the woods.
Ahead of them they could see Becky
leading the others to a clearing on the
side of a hill. Rachel and Kirsty rushed
after them.

"What an amazing adventure!" Kirsty
said breathlessly.

"It was fantastic!" Rachel agreed, her eyes shining.

When they reached the middle of the clearing, there was a fabulous view of the black night sky with the big full moon and silver stars overhead.

"And now I want to present you all with one final badge as a reward for completing the week's work," Becky announced, and she held up a big, star-shaped gold badge with *Junior Ranger* written on it.

Rachel and Kirsty were thrilled as they queued up to receive their badges with the other volunteers.

"Now you're all officially junior rangers!" Becky laughed as, bursting with pride, the girls pinned their badges to the middle of their backpacks. "I think

we should celebrate." And she began
handing out flapjacks and flasks of hot
chocolate.

"We've had *two* celebrations today,"
Rachel sighed happily, sipping her hot
chocolate. "How great is that?"

But Kirsty was staring towards the
edge of the clearing. "Look, Rachel,"
she whispered softly. "Some of our
friends are here!"

Rachel looked and saw the owl they'd met that evening, sitting in a tree. He was hooting softly, but now, of course, the girls couldn't understand what he was saying. The badger they'd seen earlier was snuffling around the bottom of the tree, and as the girls watched, the shy little fawn they'd made friends with a few days ago appeared. Then rabbits and squirrels started popping out of the undergrowth, staring at the girls with bright eyes.

"I think they've come to say goodbye!" Rachel guessed.

"And there's something else, too…" Kirsty pointed out seven tiny, twinkling lights flitting among the trees.

"Could they be the Baby Animal Rescue Fairies?" Rachel breathed excitedly. "Oh, Kirsty, I can't *wait* for our next magical adventure with our fairy friends!"

**Now it's time for Kirsty and
Rachel to help...**

Robyn the Christmas Party Fairy

Read on for a sneak peek...

"I've never seen frost looking so beautiful," said Rachel Walker, looking out of the Town Hall window.

"It's a perfect Christmas Eve morning," agreed her best friend Kirsty Tate, joining Rachel at the window.

The bright winter sun was making everything outside the window glitter. Kirsty's home town, Wetherbury, looked as if it had been frosted with white icing. The girls were spending Christmas together there, with their families.

"The party tonight is going to be

amazing." Rachel smiled. "And helping to organise it makes it even more fun."

She turned around and looked at the busy preparations that were going on in the hall. Lots of people from the community had come together to put on a special Christmas party. The girls and their families were really excited. Everyone had made something delicious to eat, and the highlight of the party was going to be a performance of a famous ballet.

Mrs Tate saw the girls over by the window and smiled at them.

Read **Robyn the Christmas Party Fairy** to find out what adventures are in store for Kirsty and Rachel!

Meet the
Baby Animal Rescue Fairies

The Baby Animal Rescue Fairies have lost all their magical items. But luckily, Kirsty and Rachel are there to save the day and make sure all baby animals in the world are safe and sound.

www.rainbowmagicbooks.co.uk

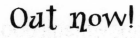

Meet the fairies, play games
and get sneak peeks at
the latest books!

www.rainbowmagicbooks.co.uk

There's fairy fun for everyone on
our wonderful website.
You'll find great activities, competitions, stories and
fairy profiles, and also a special newsletter.

Get 30% off all Rainbow Magic books at
www.rainbowmagicbooks.co.uk

Enter the code RAINBOW at the checkout.
Offer ends 31 December 2013.

Offer valid in United Kingdom and Republic of Ireland only.

Competition!

The Baby Animal Rescue Fairies have created
a special competition just for you!
In the back of each book in the series there will be
a question for you to answer.
Once you have collected all the books and all
seven answers, go online and enter the competition!

We will put all the correct entries into a draw and select
a winner to receive a special Rainbow Magic Goody Bag,
featuring lots of treats for you and your fairy friends.
The winner will also star in a new Rainbow Magic story!

**What is the name of the
Snow Fairy in the Weather
Fairies series?**

— — — — — — —

Enter online now at www.rainbowmagicbooks.co.uk

No purchase required. Only one entry per child.
Two prize draws will take place on 1st April 2014 and 2nd July 2014. Alternatively readers can
end the answer on a postcard to: Rainbow Magic, Baby Animal Rescue Fairies Competition,
Orchard Books, 338 Euston Road, London, NW1 3BH. Australian readers can write to:
Rainbow Magic, Baby Animal Rescue Fairies Competition, Hachette Children's Books,
level 17/207 Kent St, Sydney, NSW 2000. E-mail: childrens.books@hachette.com.au.
New Zealand readers should write to:
Rainbow Magic, Baby Animal Rescue Fairies Competition,
4 Whetu Place, Mairangi Bay, Auckland, NZ

Meet the
Rainbow Fairies

Collect the seven original Rainbow Fairies
to find out how the adventure began!

www.rainbowmagicbooks.co.uk